Cheryl
the Christmas Tree Fairy

With special thanks
to Rachel Elliot

To Emilia and Isabella,
with love

ORCHARD BOOKS
338 Euston Road, London NW1 3BH
Orchard Books Australia
Level 17/207 Kent Street, Sydney, NSW 2000
A Paperback Original

First published in 2010 by Orchard Books

HiT entertainment

Illustrations © Orchard Books 2010

A CIP catalogue record for this book is available
from the British Library.

ISBN 978 1 40830 915 5
1 3 5 7 9 10 8 6 4 2

Printed in Great Britain

The paper and board used in this paperback are natural recyclable
products made from wood grown in sustainable forests. The
manufacturing processes conform to the environmental regulations
of the country of origin.

Orchard Books is a division of Hachette Children's Books,
an Hachette UK company

www.hachette.co.uk

Cheryl

the Christmas Tree Fairy

by Daisy Meadows

ORCHARD BOOKS

www.rainbowmagic.co.uk

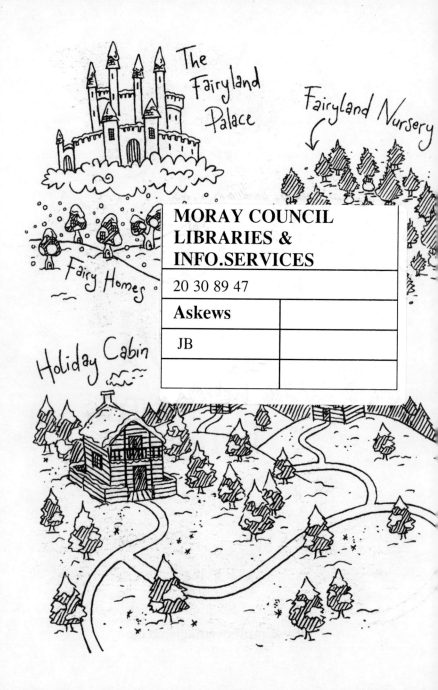

The Fairyland Palace

Fairyland Nursery

Fairy Homes

Holiday Cabin

Jack Frost's Ice Castle

Forest Clearing

Santa's Village

Reindeer Stables

Reindeer Sleigh

Christmas future, Christmas past
Let this festive magic last.
Steal away all Christmas joy
From every little girl and boy.

My Christmas will be full of glee
Thanks to the magic Christmas Tree.
Those tricksy fairies think they're clever
But I will stop their fun for ever!

The Christmas Tree

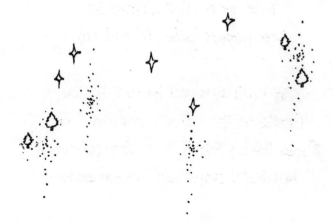

Contents

Christmas Cabin

"Just look at all the snow!" Kirsty Tate said happily.

She jumped into a powdery pile of snow and squealed in delight.

"It's so beautiful," said her best friend, Rachel Walker. "I love Lapland already!"

"And you haven't even seen inside the cabin yet," said her dad with a laugh.

"Come on, you two. You can decorate
the Christmas tree."

"Oh yes!" exclaimed Kirsty. "Each
cabin comes with its own Christmas tree,
doesn't it?"

Kirsty and Rachel's parents had been
planning this Christmas trip for months.
They had booked a big cabin in Lapland

for them all to share.

It was made of
reddish-brown
logs that
glowed in
the winter
sunshine, and
a thick layer of
snow covered the roof.

There was a sign on the door: Christmas
Cabin.

The Walkers and the Tates carried
their bags into the cosy cabin. A fire was
crackling in a woodburning stove. Large,
squashy sofas and
armchairs filled
the room, and
coloured fairy
lights were
draped around
every window.
It was beautiful!
There was just one
problem...

"Where's the tree?" asked Rachel.

Mr and Mrs Tate checked the kitchen,
Mr and Mrs Walker checked the sitting
room, and Kirsty and Rachel checked the
bedrooms. But there was no Christmas
tree in the cabin.

"It must be a mistake," said Mr Tate. "Let's go to the main office and clear it up. I'm sure they'll have a spare one for us!"

"You girls can stay here and unpack your bags," Mrs Walker told Rachel and Kirsty. "When we come back, we'll all have hot chocolate and marshmallows by the fire!"

Rachel and Kirsty agreed happily, and raced into their bedroom to unpack. Rachel had soon put all of her clothes into the wardrobe, but Kirsty was distracted.

"Look at the frost on the windows!" she said. "It looks just like lace."

Rachel joined her best friend beside
the window. The tiny panes of glass were
decorated with icy patterns.

"Everything's pretty here," she said,
"even the ice!"

"I bet Jack Frost would love it," Kirsty
smiled.

"He's the sort of frost we don't want this
Christmas!" said Rachel with a giggle.

Rachel and Kirsty were friends with all
the fairies in Fairyland. Jack Frost and
his naughty goblin servants were always
trying to make trouble, and Rachel and
Kirsty had often helped to foil their plans.

Kirsty turned to finish her unpacking, but Rachel kept gazing out of the window. Suddenly, she noticed something fluttering on the other side of the glass. The frost and snow made it difficult to see what it was. Rachel leaned closer until her nose was touching the cold pane. Were those...wings?

"Kirsty!" said Rachel in excitement. "Come and look at this!"

Kirsty rushed to join Rachel at the window. Suddenly there was a warm sizzle of golden light. It looked as if someone had lit a sparkler outside!

The frost on the window melted
away, and the girls saw a beautiful fairy
hovering outside, smiling and waving at
them. It was Holly the Christmas Fairy!

Rachel opened
the window and
Holly fluttered
inside. Her long,
dark hair was
sparkling with
snowflakes, and
she was wearing
a hooded red
dress with a feathery
white trim.

"Hello, Rachel!" she cried in her pretty,
tinkly voice. "Hi, Kirsty! I'm so glad I've
found you."

"Hello, Holly!" said Rachel in delight.

They'd had a wonderful Christmas
adventure with Holly, and had helped
her foil one of Jack Frost's mean plots.

"It's lovely to see you again," Kirsty
added. "But what are you doing in
Lapland?"

"I came to find you," said Holly. "Girls, I really need your help! Will you come with me to Fairyland – right now?"

"Of course we will!" said Rachel at once. "But what's happened?"

"I'll explain everything when we get there," Holly promised. "But we have to go now – the other winter fairies are waiting for us!"

Old Friends!

Holly flicked her wand and a stream of
sparkling red fairy dust flew out of it.
The fairy dust coiled around the girls
like ribbons, and they began to shrink.
Beautiful, gauzy wings appeared on
their backs.

"I love having wings!" Rachel
exclaimed, fluttering them in delight.

The berry-red sparkles swirled around
them faster and thicker, and the girls felt
their feet lift off the ground. Holly took
their hands as they went spinning dizzily
through the air. Then the sparkles faded
and they found themselves in Fairyland.
The emerald-green grass was hidden
underneath a white carpet and fluffy

snowflakes were
falling from
the sky.
In the
distance,
the pink
turrets
of the
Fairyland
Palace were
glittering with snow.

"Welcome to the nursery," said Holly. "This is where we look after all the baby trees in Fairyland."

Rachel and Kirsty turned around and saw that they were standing in front of a collection of pretty little trees. Best of all, hovering among the trees were their winter fairy friends!

"There's Gabriella!" cried Rachel, rushing over to hug the Snow Kingdom Fairy. "And Paige the Pantomime Fairy!"

"I'm so glad to see you both again," said Chrissie the Wish Fairy with a beaming smile.

Stella the Star Fairy threw her arms around Kirsty.

"Thank you for coming," said Gabriella. "When Cheryl told us what had happened, we thought of you straight away."

"Who's Cheryl?" asked Kirsty.

A dark-haired fairy with a sweet face and a sad expression was standing in a circle of baby pine trees. Her red dress was trimmed with white fake fur, as were her green bolero and long red boots. The neckline of her dress was decorated with a green bow, exactly the same colour as a Christmas tree. She stepped forward and gave the girls a weak smile.

"Hello," she said. "I'm Cheryl the Christmas Tree Fairy. I look after the Fairyland Christmas Tree. When the tree is decorated, it allows the festive celebrations to begin in Fairyland and the human world, and it helps to get everyone in the Christmassy mood."

"Hi," said Rachel, smiling back at the little fairy. "That sounds like a really wonderful job!"

"It is," said Cheryl. "I look forward to it very much. The Christmas Star helps everyone to feel helpful and kind at

Christmas, and the Christmas Gift helps to make sure that everyone enjoys the festivities, especially on Christmas Day. But this year, everything's gone wrong!"

"Why?" asked Rachel. "What's happened?

"It all started this morning," said Cheryl. "You see, today is a really special day. I come here to the Fairyland Nursery on this day every year. I choose one of the young pine trees to be my special Christmas Tree..."

Her eyes filled up with tears and the
other fairies put their arms
around her.

"Let's take
Rachel and
Kirsty to the
Seeing Pool
to show them
what happened,"
said Holly.

The fairies led Rachel and Kirsty to
the centre of the nursery, where tiny
green trees surrounded a glassy pool.
Cheryl waved her wand over the pool,
and the water shimmered with golden
fairy dust. A picture formed, and they
saw Cheryl and the other winter fairies
standing around a Christmas tree in
the nursery.

"I chose the Christmas Tree and all the other winter fairies joined me here for the ceremony," said Cheryl. "You see, when I have chosen the tree, I say a magic spell. As soon as the spell is cast, everyone in Fairyland and the human world starts to feel happy and Christmassy."

Rachel and Kirsty stood beside Cheryl, wondering just what had happened to upset her so much...

Jack Frost Attacks!

In the picture, Cheryl waved her wand over the tree and it began to sparkle. Then she placed a shimmering purple and pink star on top of the tree.

"That's the Christmas Star," Cheryl whispered. "And look, that's the Christmas Gift."

In the Seeing Pool, Rachel and Kirsty saw Cheryl put a present under the tree. It was wrapped in red paper with a Christmas tree pattern and finished with a sprig of holly.

"I have to give a final wave of my wand to complete the Christmas magic," said Cheryl. "But before I could do that... look what happened!"

Rachel and Kirsty gazed into the pool. They saw Cheryl lift her arm to wave her wand. Then there was a big blue flash like a bolt of lightning! When the light cleared, the winter fairies were scattered around the nursery as if someone had knocked them down.

Worst of all, Jack Frost and three of his goblin servants were standing beside the Christmas Tree! Jack Frost glared at the fairies and stroked his icy beard.

"You silly little fairies have had your silly little Christmas Tree ceremony for the last time," he cackled. "Seize them!"

The goblin nearest the tree grabbed the Christmas Star.

"No!" cried Cheryl, raising her wand.

Jack Frost sent a lightning bolt that knocked the wand out of her hand.

"Not so fast, little fairy!" he jeered.
The second goblin picked up the
Christmas Gift, and the third goblin
stretched his arms around the Christmas
Tree and tried to lift it.

"OW!" he
hollerd as
pine needles
pricked his
face and
arms. "Ooh!
Ouch!
Argh!"
"Stop
complaining!"
snapped Jack Frost.

"Please stop!" cried Cheryl. "If you
take these things away, Christmas will be
spoiled for everyone."

"Not for me." Jack Frost declared triumphantly. "And I'm the one that matters! I'm sick of having the same old Christmas as everyone else. This year, my Christmas is going to be the best in the whole world!"

"How can you enjoy it if it makes other people miserable?" asked Cheryl.

Jack Frost glared at her and then cackled.

"That just makes it even better," he told her.

"I won't let you get away with this," Cheryl said.

"You don't have a choice," Jack Frost snarled.

He waved his wand and all three goblins disappeared – together with the magical Christmas objects!

"No!" cried Cheryl.

"You'll never see your precious tree, star or gift again," Jack Frost declared. "You pesky fairies think you're so clever, but I've been too cunning for you this time!"

With a final cackle, Jack Frost waved his wand and disappeared. The picture in the Seeing Pool faded, and Rachel and Kirsty turned to Cheryl.

"We won't let Jack Frost get away with this," said Rachel in a determined voice.

"He's not as cunning as he thinks he is," Kirsty added. "I bet we can work out where he's hidden the tree, the star *and* the gift."

"But there are only three days until Christmas," said Cheryl, looking worried. "There's so little time!"

Rachel and Kirsty put their arms around the little fairy.

"Then we'd better get started straight away!" said Rachel.

Gloomy Goblins

Suddenly, Paige gave a loud gasp.

"The king and queen will be wondering what's happened," she said.

"You should all go and tell them what Jack Frost has done," said Cheryl.

"But we want to help you," said Stella.

"I've got Rachel and Kirsty," said Cheryl, smiling at the girls. "The king and queen will need all of you to help with the other Christmas preparations."

The other winter fairies hugged them goodbye and wished them luck, and then flew off to find the king and queen. Cheryl looked at the girls.

"I wish I felt as confident as you," she said. "But I have no idea where to start looking."

Rachel frowned. "I think we should start with the most obvious place," she said. "Maybe Jack Frost has taken everything to the Ice Castle."

Cheryl gave a little shiver. "It's a horrible place," she said. "Are you sure that you want to help me with this?"

"Of course!" Kirsty exclaimed bravely. "Besides, we've been inside the Ice Castle before. We're not scared!"

"Then let's go!" said Cheryl.

They fluttered their wings and rose up into the air together. As they flew towards the Ice Castle, the air grew colder and dark clouds gathered overhead. They zipped over a forest where the treetops were dusted with powdery snow.

"Look, Rachel," said Kirsty, pointing at the trees. "They look like cakes covered in icing sugar!"

Rachel looked down too, and suddenly she spotted something.

"What's that?" she asked, pausing and hovering in midair.

Kirsty and Cheryl peered down through the snowy trees. In a clearing, almost hidden from view, they  could see three small, green figures sitting in a circle. They were pointing at each other with their long, bony fingers.

"Goblins," said Cheryl. "We must be close to the Ice Castle."

"It looks as if they're having an argument," said Kirsty, thoughtfully.

"Goblins are so bad-tempered," Cheryl
remarked. "Come on, let's get to the
castle."

"Just a minute," said Kirsty. "I've got a
funny feeling about those goblins. Let's go
down and find out what they're up to."

The three friends swooped silently
downwards. They landed on a tree branch
above the goblins. Sure enough, the
goblins were in the middle of a big row.

"It's not my fault!" a plump goblin was saying. "I thought *you* were watching it!"

He jabbed his finger into the belly of a wart-covered goblin, who gave a yell of pain.

"I was watching out for pesky fairies!" he shrieked. "*He* was supposed to be guarding the tree!"

He pointed at the smallest goblin, who was wearing a bobble hat.

"Don't pick on me!" exclaimed the smallest goblin.

When the warty goblin mentioned the tree, the girls clutched each other in excitement.

"Could it be *my* tree?" Cheryl whispered.

"Oh, I really hope so!" said Rachel.

"It must be," said Kirsty with confidence. "Why else would the goblins be guarding a tree?"

The smallest goblin shoved the others to get their attention.

"Shut up, you idiots!" he said. "We need to work out which one is the magic tree, before Jack Frost turns our noses into icicles."

When he said this, all the goblins put their hands over their noses and looked scared.

"We know it's somewhere in this forest," said the plump goblin. "Maybe we should just guard all the trees."

"Don't be stupid," snapped the warty goblin. "There are hundreds of trees in this gloomy forest and there are only three of us!"

"Well I don't hear you coming up with a better plan!" shrieked the plump goblin, clenching his fists.

The two goblins hurled themselves at each other and rolled around the clearing, wrestling and yelling.

"Of course," said Cheryl in a low voice. "As soon as the tree is taken out of the nursery, it loses its sparkle. It looks like an ordinary tree again!"

The Smell of Success!

"Can *you* tell which one is the magic Christmas Tree?" asked Rachel.

"I can cast a spell to make it sparkle again," said Cheryl, nodding.

"First we have to get the goblins out of the clearing," Kirsty realised. "Cheryl, get your wand ready. I've got an idea!"

Kirsty, Rachel and Cheryl flew high above the treetops.

"We have to keep the goblins away
from us," Kirsty said. "Cheryl, can you use
your magic to lure them away?"

"Of course, but what will tempt them
away?" said Cheryl.

The girls thought hard.

"I know!" said Rachel suddenly. "If you
conjure up a wonderful
smell of food, I'm sure
they'll try to find
where it's coming
from! We know how
greedy goblins are."

Cheryl immediately
flicked her wand and a swirl of steam
came out of it. The steam drifted down to
the goblins in a curling ribbon. It smelled
like hot mince pies and rich Christmas
pudding. It made the girls feel hungry!

The goblins raised their noses into the
air as the ribbon of steam passed by.

"Food!" exclaimed the plump goblin,
scrambling to his feet.

"That smells *so*
good!" said the
warty goblin.

Cheryl sent
the ribbon of
steam away
through the
trees, and the

three goblins followed
it eagerly. Then she muttered a few magic
words and waved her wand. Silver glitter
floated down and landed on the treetops.
The girls scanned the area eagerly, but
they saw nothing.

"It's not here," said Cheryl.

"Let's try another area," Rachel
suggested.

Cheryl used the ribbon of delicious-
smelling steam to send the goblins
further away from them. Then she waved
her wand again. This time, they saw
something glittering far below.

"Oh, please let it be my Christmas
Tree!" Cheryl exclaimed.

They zoomed down into the forest.
Among a thick cluster of tall pines, they
saw a beautiful, sparkling Christmas Tree.

"We've found it!" squealed Rachel in
excitement.

Cheryl waved
her wand
over the tree,
but nothing
happened.

"That should have sent it back to the nursery!" cried Cheryl in alarm. "Jack Frost must have put a sticking spell on it!"

"Can't you break it?" said Kirsty.

"Not by myself," said Cheryl, looking very upset.

"Can we help?" asked Rachel.

"I have to make the tree's magic stronger than the spell," Cheryl explained. "We'll have to make a circle around the tree and then think about how much we love Christmas. But it really needs more than three people. I don't know if we'll be strong enough."

"Let's try!" said Kirsty, holding out her hands.

They stood around the tree and held hands, making a circle. Then they closed their eyes and thought about Christmas as hard as they could. Rachel thought about Christmas pudding and wrapping Christmas presents. Kirsty thought about singing carols and having fun with her family. They felt a rush of warmth passing through their hands.

"That's it!" cried Cheryl, waving her wand again.

This time there was a loud POUFF! and the tree disappeared in a puff of red and gold fairy dust. It had worked!

"Hurray!" said Cheryl. "Now for the goblins."

She drew the ribbon of steam back to her wand. A few seconds later, the girls heard the swish of leaves and the snapping of twigs. Then the goblins pushed through the bushes in front of them.

"Fairies!" gasped the bobble-hatted goblin.

"Have you greedy things eaten all the food?" asked the plump goblin suspiciously.

"No, but we've found the magic Christmas Tree and sent it back to the Fairyland Nursery," said Kirsty, folding her arms.

The goblins groaned.

"We're in big trouble now!" wailed the warty one.

Cheryl waved her wand and a plate of mince pies appeared in front of the goblins.

"I'm sorry you're so cold and hungry," she said. "No one should be hungry at Christmas, not even naughty creatures!"

 The goblins fell on the mince pies, snaffling them up as fast as they could. Cheryl hugged

Rachel and Kirsty and gave them a beaming smile.

"Thank you," she said. "If it hadn't been for you, I would never have spotted the goblins in the forest."

"We're so glad we could help!" said Rachel.

"I'm going to the palace to tell the king and queen that we found my Christmas Tree," said Cheryl. "It's time for you to go home. But I'll see you again soon!"

Cheryl waved her wand and the girls were surrounded by a misty whirl of golden fairy dust. When it cleared, they were back in Christmas Cabin!

"Girls," called Mrs Tate from the sitting room. "We've got the tree!"

"There are some wonderful decorations for you to use!" added Mrs Walker. "And we've just made some hot chocolate."

Rachel looked at Kirsty with shining eyes, and Kirsty gave a happy sigh.

"A tree to decorate, hot chocolate with marshmallows and a fairy adventure," she said. "What a magical start to our Christmas holiday!"

The Christmas Star

Contents

Santa's Village

The following morning, the girls and their parents were up bright and early. They had decided to take a husky ride to a special place called Santa's Village.

"Are you looking forward to the ride, girls?" asked Mr Walker.

Rachel and Kirsty nodded eagerly.

"I dreamed about huskies all night!" said Kirsty, laughing.

"I dreamed about Santa's Village," added Rachel. "There's a toy factory, a gift shop and reindeer for sleigh rides. The people who work there must be so lovely!"

"Maybe they won't be lovely if we can't find the Christmas Star," Kirsty whispered to her friend in a worried voice. "The star is what helps everyone to feel helpful and kind, remember?"

Jack Frost and his goblins had stolen three enchanted items from Cheryl the Christmas Tree Fairy. Kirsty and Rachel had helped her to find the magical Christmas Tree, but they still had to find the Christmas Star and the Christmas Gift, and time was running out. There were only two days left until Christmas.

"Let's go, girls!" said Mr Tate.

Their guide was waiting for them outside. When the girls saw the husky dogs, they gasped in delight.

"They're so beautiful!" said Kirsty,
her breath hovering mistily in the air.

Rachel and Kirsty loved the dogs'
snow-tipped fur coats and bright,
intelligent blue eyes. Everyone climbed
into the sled and snuggled together under
warm blankets.

"Mush!" cried the guide, and the
huskies set off.

The dogs sped over silent, white expanses, past snow-clad pine trees, grazing reindeer and cosy log cabins. They were going so fast that the cold wind took their breath away, and no one could speak a word. But Kirsty's hand found Rachel's under the thick blankets, and they smiled at each other, their eyes sparkling.

The ride was over much too soon.
The huskies slowed down as they arrived
in Santa's Village, and the sled stopped
outside a very large building. It was
decorated with coloured lights, and
had an arched sign over the door:

The girls and their parents jumped out
of the sled and went to say
thank you to the guide
and the dogs. Then
Mr Tate looked at
his watch.
"Why don't you
girls have a look inside
Santa's Workshop, while
we wander around the gift shop?" he said.

"Then we can go for a reindeer ride!"

Rachel and Kirsty nodded and ran up the path to the door of Santa's Workshop. A man dressed as an elf opened the door for them. He was wearing a pine-green outfit with red trim.

"Welcome to Santa's Workshop," he said with a beaming smile. "This is where we make toys for children all over the world. We're especially proud of the beautiful wooden toys that our carpenters make."

71

The girls stepped through the door and stopped in wonder and astonishment. The workshop seemed much, much bigger on the inside! Huge machines whizzed and whirred all around them, letting out long whistles and whooshing coloured sparks into the air. Dozens of people dressed as elves rushed around busily.

"Go ahead," said the man who was holding the door for them. "Just follow the silver arrows painted on the floor, and you'll see all the toys being made and then visit the reindeer. You might even see Santa, if you're lucky!"

Rachel and Kirsty walked on, following the trail of silver arrows that were painted on the workshop floor.

They came to a long table where several carpenters were sitting in a row. Each one was concentrating hard on the toy he or she was making. Further down the line, more people dressed as elves were painting wooden toys in bright colours.

Kirsty's eyes shone as she turned to her best friend, but Rachel was frowning.

"What's wrong?" asked Kirsty.

Rachel pointed under the table, to where two very small elves were crouching. They were tying some of the carpenters' shoelaces together!

"Those naughty elves!" Kirsty exclaimed.

"Those aren't elves," said Rachel, as the culprits turned to each other, showing long, green noses. "They're *goblins!*"

Cheryl to the Rescue!

"Oh no!" cried Kirsty. "What are we going to do?"

At that moment, a large machine beside them let off a loud whistle. Then there was a whoosh of red sparkles, and Cheryl shot out of the machine!

"Hello, girls!" she said.

"Thank goodness you're here," said
Rachel. "There are two goblins causing
trouble over there!"

She quickly explained what had
happened, but when they turned back
to the table, the goblins had disappeared.
All the carpenters' shoelaces were tied
together.

"I'd better fix that before someone gets
hurt," said Cheryl, looking worried.

She waved her wand and said:

"Foil this naughty goblin plot –
Untie each tangle and each knot!
Laces all should loop and show
On every foot a perfect bow."

The girls watched as the shoelaces untied
themselves from each
other and formed
neat bows.

"I can't
believe the
goblins are
here," said
Rachel.

"They're definitely up to
no good," said Cheryl. "Let's follow them
and find out what they're up to!"

Cheryl tucked herself under a lock of Kirsty's hair and the girls followed the silver arrows deeper into the workshop, looking left and right for the goblins.

"Over there!" Kirsty exclaimed.

Two figures in green uniforms were kneeling down over a blue-and-red machine, peering into the engine. One of them was holding a spanner; the other had a hammer.

"We have to stop them," cried Rachel. "They're going to break the machine!"

The girls dashed across and pulled them
away from the machine. Then, to their
horror, they saw two surprised human
faces staring at them!

"We're so sorry!" said
Kirsty, her cheeks
scarlet with
embarrassment.
"We thought
you were...
someone else."

The girls
backed away and
rejoined the silver
arrows. They walked
further into the workshop,
and then Cheryl gasped.

"I see them," she cried. "There
they are!"

There was no doubt this time. The girls could see the goblins' green faces. They were standing in a quiet corner beside

a crate full of toys, whispering to each other.

"Come on," said Rachel. "Let's find out what they're saying."

The girls darted over to the other side of the crate and edged their way around it until they could hear the goblins' voices.

"It's fun playing tricks on these silly people," the first goblin was saying. "What shall we do next?"

"Playing tricks isn't the only reason we're here," said the second goblin. "Look what I've got."

He lifted the hat of his elf costume and the girls gasped. Underneath the hat was something purple and shining.

"The Christmas Star!" gasped Cheryl.

"What are you doing with that?" asked the first goblin, his eyes almost popping out of his head.

"Jack Frost's too mean to find a decent star for our tree," said the second goblin. "This one's rubbish!"

"What's wrong with it?" asked the first goblin.

"It's too small," grumbled the second goblin. "I want an enormous star for our tree, and there's bound to be a better one here. They make all sorts of pretty things in this place. I stole it from Jack Frost so that we can do a swap!"

"Oh my goodness," whispered Kirsty. "The goblins don't know that the star's got magical powers!"

Find Those Goblins!

The girls stared at each other in astonishment and alarm.

"How are we going to get the star back?" asked Cheryl.

"I've got a plan," said Rachel, her eyes shining. "They're here to replace the star with something bigger. If we can find something they like, we might be able to persuade them to swap it!"

"I could make a star decoration that they'll love," said Cheryl, tapping her wand thoughtfully against  her cheek. "It will have to be something big and colourful to please the goblins."

"Good idea," said Kirsty. "But first we have to find them!"

She pointed to where the goblins had been standing. They had disappeared again!

"I wish they'd stop doing that," said Rachel. "Come on, we have to find them!"

The girls hurried through the workshop. They peered around machines, under tables and inside crates of toys.

They looked hard at all the workers they passed, and they even checked in the kitchen at the back of the workshop. But there was no sign of the naughty goblins.

Suddenly they heard someone yell, "What do you think you're doing?"

The girls looked at each other in excitement.

"I bet that's the goblins up to mischief!" Kirsty exclaimed. "Quick, let's find out what's going on."

They ran over to where the shout had come from. A few people in elf outfits were standing in a huddle, their hands on their hips. Above their heads hung a sign: Testing Area. Each of them was wearing a badge that said 'Toy Tester'. Rachel and Kirsty peered over their shoulders.

One of the goblins was sitting on a wooden tricycle that was much too small for him. He was pedalling around in circles. There was a long piece of string attached to the back of the tricycle, and tied to it were wooden dolls, wooden blocks and a toy train. The toys were crashing and bouncing along behind the tricycle, and the goblin giggled as he pedalled faster and faster.

"Stop!" cried the toy testers. "You're breaking the toys!"

The second goblin was waving a cricket bat around in one hand and throwing tennis balls into the air with the other. None of the helpers could get near him.

"Wheeee!" shouted the second goblin.

He whacked a tennis ball with the cricket bat. It soared into the air, hit the ceiling and bounced off the head of one of the toy testers.

"Ouch!" he cried, rubbing his head.

"We have to stop them!" Rachel exclaimed.

She rushed forwards and stood on the string that was trailing from the back of the tricycle. She dug her heels into the ground. The goblin gave a screech of anger and toppled off.

"You horrible girl!" he squealed, leaping to his feet and hopping up and down in fury. "You've spoiled my fun!"

"We just want to talk to you—" Rachel began.

But the goblin darted behind a table piled high with toys, and disappeared. Meanwhile, Kirsty had dashed towards the other goblin.

"Stop hitting those tennis balls," she pleaded. "You'll hurt someone!"

"Yah boo sucks!" retorted the goblin. He stuck out his tongue, blew a raspberry and then threw down the cricket bat and raced after his companion.

Goblins in Danger!

While the workers began to clear up the mess, Rachel and Kirsty set off after the goblins. Cheryl was still hiding under Kirsty's hair. Ahead, they saw three girls in elf outfits standing together. Each of them was holding a clipboard and looking very upset.

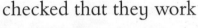

"Has something happened?" asked Kirsty, hurrying up to them.

"Someone has spoiled our checklists," said one of the girls. "We have to check that all the toys are safe to go into the gift shop. We tick little boxes when we've checked that they work and they're made well. But someone has put ticks in *all* the boxes on our sheets. We can't tell which are real and which aren't, so we'll have to start from scratch!"

"That's so mean," said Rachel.

"That's goblins," muttered Kirsty under her breath.

Suddenly, Rachel caught a glimpse
of a green foot as it disappeared around
a corner.

"What's over there?" she asked the elves.

"Just the Reindeer Barn," the girl

replied.
Kirsty and
Rachel
exchanged
a worried
glance.

"If those
goblins upset the
reindeer, no one will be
able to have a sleigh ride today," Kirsty
exclaimed. "We have to stop them."

The girls ran over to where the goblins
had been, and found a large wooden
door. The sign on the door said:

Reindeer Barn.
Please keep this door shut.
(And no extra carrots for Rudolf.
He's on a diet.)

The door was swinging open.

"Oh no," said Rachel. "I think we're too late."

They stepped into the barn. The floor was covered with straw, and the barn was lined with empty bays. Each bay had a different name printed on it.

"Dancer... Prancer... Rudolf..." Kirsty read aloud. "This is where the reindeer live – but where are they?"

"They're out on a sleigh ride," said a voice behind them.

The girls whirled around and saw the man who had let them in to the workshop.

"I'm sure you'll see them another time," he said. "But this door is supposed to be kept closed."

The girls smiled at him and went back into the workshop.

"That's a relief," said Rachel. "The goblins must have found the barn empty."

"But where did they go next?" asked Kirsty.

"I think I know!" said Cheryl, flying out from under Kirsty's hair. "Look at that."

She pointed at the floor. There were a few wispy strands of straw leading away from the barn door.

"Let's follow them," said Rachel.

Cheryl fluttered ahead of them and they followed the trail of straw. As they hurried along, they heard a hum of chatter that grew louder and louder.

The straw trail ran out, but by that time the voices were leading them along.

They turned a corner and saw another group of angry-looking people staring at a big red-and-gold machine. The goblins were dancing around on the edge of the machine!

"Come down at once!" the head carpenter demanded. But the goblins kept on jumping around, sticking their tongues out at the workers surrounding them.

Suddenly one of the goblins wobbled, shrieked and clutched at the other. They both lost their balance – and tumbled into the machine!

Goblin Gifts

The machine let out a series of whistles and beeps. There were some loud clunks.

"Oh no!" cried Rachel. "We have to rescue them!"

"What sort of machine is it?" asked Kirsty, turning to the head carpenter.

"It's an automatic wrapping machine," he replied. "It can wrap any present, any size."

"Will they be all right?" asked Rachel.

"They'll be fine," said the head carpenter, looking stern. "Just a bit shocked. Perhaps it will teach them a lesson!"

A large chute opened at the base of the machine, and two goblin-shaped presents popped out. They were wrapped in shiny Christmas paper.

Rachel and Kirsty hurried over and tore the paper at the knobbly end of each present. Green, angry goblin faces appeared.

"Let us go!" they demanded, struggling against the wrapping. "It's not funny!"

"It *is* quite funny," said Rachel, stifling a giggle.

"We're not letting you go until you've listened to what we have to say," said Kirsty.

The goblins grumbled and wriggled, but they couldn't get away. Rachel and Kirsty kneeled down in front of them, and Cheryl fluttered onto Rachel's knee.

"I should have guessed," muttered the first goblin when he saw her. "Bothersome fairies!"

"Listen," said Rachel. "We want to help you. We overheard you saying that you want a bigger decoration for the top of your tree. Cheryl will make one for you, if you'll swap your star for it."

The goblins narrowed their eyes suspiciously.

"Why would you do that?" asked the second goblin.

"Because we like your star," said Kirsty truthfully. "And it's Christmas. People are supposed to be extra nice to each other at Christmas."

"I could make you the best tree decoration you've ever seen," said Cheryl.

The goblins looked at each other and
then nodded.

"All right," they said. "Show us."

Rachel and Kirsty undid the rest of the
wrapping paper while Cheryl waved her
wand. Golden fairy dust streamed from
the tip of her wand and zigzagged into
the shape of a large gold star. Red, blue
and yellow jewels sparkled at its centre.
It hung in the air in front of the goblins.
Their mouths fell open in wonder.

"Well?" asked Rachel, holding her
breath.

"It's the most beautiful decoration I've ever seen!" gasped the first goblin.

The second goblin lifted his hat, took out the magic Christmas Star and handed it to Cheryl. She waved her wand again and returned the Christmas Star to its fairy size.

"I don't know how to thank you, girls," she said.

"Just return the star to the Christmas Tree," said Kirsty. "Then everyone will start feeling helpful and kind!"

"And that's what Christmas is all about," Cheryl said.

She blew them a kiss and disappeared in a flurry of fairy dust.

Moments later, the girls felt a warm glow pass through their bodies. It gave them a contented, happy feeling. They just wanted to smile at everyone!

"That must mean that the Christmas Star is back where it belongs," said Rachel.

The first goblin tucked the huge star under his arm and rubbed his hands together.

"Time to get back to the Ice Castle," he said.

"Wait a minute," said the second goblin. "Maybe we should stay around here and help the elves to tidy up."

"Oh," the first goblin said. "OK. We did make a lot of mess."

Rachel and Kirsty watched in amazement as the goblins hurried off to help the elves.

"Well," said Kirsty, finding her voice at last. "I suppose the Christmas Star must have affected the goblins as well."

"And that's what I call powerful magic!" Rachel smiled.

The Christmas Gift

Contents

News from Fairyland

"Could you pass me the gold ribbon, please?" Rachel asked Kirsty. "I want to make Mum's present look extra-special."

It was Christmas Eve, and the girls were busy wrapping presents in their room. It was dark, but they hadn't closed the curtains yet. Fairy lights twinkled in the window, and fluffy flakes of snow were falling outside.

"Christmas in Lapland is almost as magical as Fairyland," said Kirsty, handing the gold ribbon to her best friend and staring out of the window.

"I hope that Christmas *will* be magical," Rachel  said, tying the ribbon around the little box of perfume and making it spiral down in curly strands. "It will be spoiled here *and* in Fairyland if we can't find the Christmas Gift."

The girls were enjoying a Christmas holiday in Lapland, but as soon as they arrived, Jack Frost and his goblins had started causing trouble.

They had taken Cheryl the Christmas
Tree Fairy's special magical items.
With the help of Kirsty and Rachel
she had found the Christmas Tree and
the beautiful Christmas Star, but the
Christmas Gift was still missing.

"The Christmas Gift helps to make sure
that everyone enjoys the festivities," Kirsty
remembered. "Oh Rachel, I hope Jack
Frost doesn't ruin Christmas Day, or the
midnight carol concert!"

"Me too," said Rachel, starting to
wrap her dad's present, which was a new
cycling helmet. "It'll be so much fun!"

Rachel and Kirsty were very excited about Christmas Day, and the outdoor concert the next evening. There were going to be carols, and the girls would be allowed to stay up late to take part.

"Somehow we've got to find that Christmas Gift, no matter what!" said Rachel in a determined voice.

Suddenly, Kirsty gasped and pointed at the silver wrapping paper that Rachel was using. Golden sparkles were dancing around the edges of the paper.

"Those are fairy sparkles!" Kirsty exclaimed.

"You're right!" cried Rachel, letting go of the paper.

The girls watched in delight as the paper wrapped itself around the cycling helmet box. Silvery ribbons curled around it and tied themselves into beautiful bows.

Then there was a puff of golden fairy dust, and Cheryl appeared in the midst of it, flying upwards until she was hovering face to face with the girls.

"Hello girls. I know where the Christmas Gift is!" she sighed.

"That's wonderful!" said Rachel, clapping her hands together in excitement.

"So where is it?" asked Kirsty eagerly.

Both girls thought it strange that Cheryl didn't seem happy about the news. Her eyes looked worried and she wasn't smiling.

"I've been searching high and low
in Fairyland," she said. "Everyone has
joined in – even the king and queen.
We've looked under every toadstool and
investigated every bird's nest. No one has
been able to find the Christmas Gift."

"Does that mean it's here in the human
world?" asked Rachel.

Cheryl shook
her head.

"I would know
if it had left
Fairyland because
of my strong
connection with it,"
she said. "This morning we
searched beneath the last blade of grass,
and Queen Titania said that there is only
one place it can be...the Ice Castle."

123

Rachel and Kirsty exchanged worried looks. They had been in Jack Frost's chilling domain before, and it was cold and dangerous.

"Will you help me again, girls?" asked Cheryl, clasping her hands together. "I know it's a big favour to ask...but will you come and search the Ice Castle with me?"

Rachel and Kirsty didn't hesitate. There was only one answer they could give.

"Yes!" they said together.

A Snowy Disguise!

Cheryl waved her wand, and a burst of golden fairy dust exploded from it like a tiny firework. It coiled around the girls' ankles and spiralled up around their bodies, until they were glimmering with gold sparkles. Gauzy wings sprouted from their backs as they shrank to fairy size.

The golden coils became whirling
hoops of light, spinning around them.
Their bedroom vanished in a blur, and
when the coils disappeared, the girls
found themselves standing in the forest
outside Jack Frost's
castle.

"Wow!"
said Kirsty.
"I think
that was
the fastest
trip to
Fairyland
ever!"

"We have
to be quick," said
Cheryl in an urgent whisper. "There are
only a few hours of Christmas Eve left.

If midnight strikes before I have the Christmas Gift, it will be too late and no one will enjoy Christmas Day."

"But how are we going to get inside the castle?" asked Rachel. "There are bound to be guards on duty, and they won't allow us to fly in."

Kirsty looked up into the darkening sky. Snowflakes were cascading down.

"I've got an idea!" she said, her eyes sparkling. "Cheryl, could you disguise us as snowflakes? Then we could fly straight into the central courtyard, and the goblin guards wouldn't suspect a thing!"

"That's a great idea!" said Cheryl.

The three friends zipped up into the sky and hovered above the snowy courtyard at the centre of the castle. Sure enough, there were several goblin guards on sentry duty. They were marching up and down, looking very important.

Cheryl tapped Rachel and Kirsty with her wand, and then touched it against her own dark head.

Instantly, they all shrank to the size of
snowflakes, and were coated in white
from head to toe, with
sparkly crowns
on their
heads!

"We
look as if
someone's
wrapped
us in white
lace!" giggled
Rachel.

The girls flew
downwards, making sure that they moved
at the same speed as the snowflakes.
Rachel was remembering the time they
had visited the castle with Belle the
Birthday Fairy.

"Head towards that corridor," she whispered, pointing at a dark archway in the courtyard wall. "That leads to the Great Hall – we could start our search there."

They landed under the archway. The goblin guards were still marching around the courtyard. They were wearing colourful woolly hats and scarves to protect them from the cold.

"Come on, before they notice us!" whispered Cheryl, her breath hanging in the icy air.

As the three friends fluttered into the corridor, their snowflake disguises melted away and they returned to fairy size. They flew quickly to the Great Hall, but the doors were wide open and it was empty.

"We have to keep looking," Kirsty whispered.

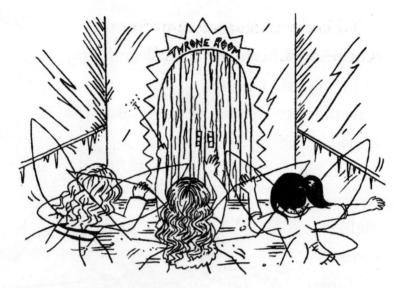

They flew further along the corridor, deep into the castle. At last they reached another set of large double doors. The words 'Throne Room' were carved above them.

"Listen!" said Rachel, putting her ear to the door.

Someone was speaking in low, grumbling tones.

"I'd know that voice anywhere!"
Rachel said. "It's Jack Frost!"

Jack Frost's Mistake

Cheryl tapped her wand on the door and it slowly creaked open. The girls peered around it.

"There he is!" gasped Cheryl.

Jack Frost was sitting with one leg hooked over the arm of the throne and his spiky chin resting on his hand. He was staring at a small, sad-looking Christmas tree. Its only decorations were several large icicles and the huge star that Cheryl had made for the goblins.

"That poor little Christmas tree is so unloved," said Cheryl with a sigh.

"But look what's underneath it!" cried Rachel in excitement.

Under the drooping branches of the tree was the Christmas Gift!

"Those stupid goblins have ruined my Christmas *again*," Jack Frost was muttering to himself. "Can't they do anything right? They lost the Christmas Tree, *gave away* the Christmas Star, and now they've done something to the Christmas Gift to  stop it working. I'm sick of the sight of them!"

"What is he talking about?" asked Kirsty in a low voice. "The Christmas Gift looks all right to me."

"I don't know," said Cheryl, lifting her chin bravely, "but I'm going to find out."

She fluttered into the middle of the
Throne Room. Rachel and Kirsty flew
close behind her. Jack Frost was still
staring at the tree, his eyebrows knitted
together in an icy frown. He hadn't
spotted them.

"Jack Frost!" said Cheryl loudly.

Jack Frost's head whipped around to

face them, and
his lips curled
when he
saw the
three
fairies.
"You!"
he snarled.
"How did
you get into
my castle?"

"We've come to ask you to return the Christmas Gift," said Rachel bravely.

"It's no use to you," Kirsty added.

"Tell me how to make it work!" Jack Frost roared, leaping to his feet.

Cheryl looked at the girls in confusion, and Jack Frost gave a bellow of rage.

"No fairy tricks!" he shouted.

He pointed his wand and a volley of ice bolts came hurtling towards them!

"Duck!" cried Cheryl.

The three girls scattered and the ice bolts just missed them.

"Make it work or I'll turn you all into tiny ice sculptures and use you as ornaments!" Jack Frost snarled.

"The Christmas Gift can only do its job when it's in the Fairyland nursery, underneath the Christmas Tree," Cheryl explained, looking puzzled.

"You're lying!" Jack Frost hissed. "You just want to keep all the presents for yourself!"

"Fairies don't lie," said Cheryl indignantly.

"I don't know what you're talking about. The Christmas Gift doesn't bring presents."

Jack Frost sat down on his throne with a heavy thump, and his mouth fell open.

"What?" he said.

"I think I understand," said Rachel, thoughtfully. "Jack Frost thought that the Christmas Gift would bring him lots of presents – that's why he wanted it."

Cheryl fluttered closer to the throne.

"That's not what the Christmas Gift does," she said gently. "You made a mistake. Its job is to make sure that everyone has a happy time on Christmas Day."

"Then it should give me hundreds of presents!" Jack Frost shouted.

"Presents can't make you happy," said Cheryl. "It's the magic and warmth of Christmas that does that."

Rachel and Kirsty fluttered closer.

"Please give us back the Christmas Gift," said Kirsty. "Then everyone can have a happy Christmas."

Jack Frost looked suspicious.

"Even me?" he asked.

"Yes," said Cheryl. "I promise that if you give me the Christmas Gift, you'll have the jolliest Christmas you've ever had."

The girls held their breath. Would Jack Frost agree? He raised his wand and Rachel clutched Kirsty's arm. What was he going to do?

A Magical Invitation

Muttering a spell, Jack Frost pointed his wand at the Christmas Gift.

It rose into the air and floated towards Cheryl, shrinking as it moved. By the time it landed in her arms, it had shrunk to fairy size. Jack Frost lowered his wand.

"Thank you," said Cheryl. "I'll return the Christmas Gift to its rightful place under the Christmas Tree. Then you will see how wonderful Christmas can be!"

"All right," he growled. "But just in case you're lying to me, those other two can stay here until you get back."

"That's not fair." gasped Cheryl. "I told you; I'm not lying!"

"It's OK," said Rachel. "We'll wait for you here."

"Aren't you scared?" asked Cheryl in a low voice.

"Not when we're together," said Kirsty, linking arms with her best friend.

"I think you're both very brave," said Cheryl, blowing them both a kiss.

She disappeared in a flash of golden sparkles, and Jack Frost glowered at Rachel and Kirsty.

"If she doesn't come back, I'm going to lock you both in my deepest dungeon," he said.

Rachel glanced at the tall windows
and shivered. It was dark outside, but the
moon's rays were shining on the swirling
snowflakes. Then she saw something
coming rapidly towards the window,
flying through the snow.

"Kirsty, look!" she exclaimed.

The object got closer and closer, curving
down through the sky.

"It's going to crash through the window!" Kirsty cried.

Jack Frost dived behind his throne and the girls covered their faces, expecting to hear shattering glass, but all they heard was the tinkling of countless bells. They opened their eyes. Jack Frost was cowering behind  his throne, but Kirsty and Rachel clapped their hands happily.

Standing in the middle of the Throne
Room, draped in red velvet and tiny silver
bells, was Santa's sleigh! Nine reindeer
were stamping their hooves on the
flagstones and shaking the snow off their
furry coats.

"Greetings, Jack Frost!" said one of the
reindeer in a gruff, dignified voice.

Jack Frost stepped out from behind his throne, adjusting his robes and clearing his throat.

"What do you want?" he demanded rudely.

"Santa sent us," said the reindeer. "He wants to thank you for returning the Christmas Gift to its rightful place.

He would like to invite you to help him deliver the presents this year."

Jack Frost paused for a minute, his hand resting on his icy chin. Then he let out a little whoop of excitement and capered around his throne, chuckling and grinning.

"I've never seen him look so happy!" said Rachel with a giggle.

"Santa sends his greetings to you, too,
Kirsty and Rachel," said the reindeer.
"He knows what a great help you have
been to the fairies."

Before they could
reply, Rachel
and Kirsty
heard a
whooshing
sound
above
them.
Golden fairy
dust began to
rain downwards
from the ceiling. The girls gasped in
delight. Everywhere the fairy dust
touched was transformed before
their eyes.

155

Silver and gold decorations spanned
the ceiling, candles flickered in the
windows, and sprigs of holly were pinned
to the walls. Best of all, the sad-looking
Christmas tree became tall and bushy,
draped with tinsel and glistening with
baubles. The star glistened at the top.

Cheryl the Christmas Tree Fairy was hovering in the centre of it all, smiling with her wand held aloft.

"Merry Christmas, everyone!" she exclaimed.

The Perfect Christmas

The Throne Room doors burst open and a crowd of goblins scampered in, wearing party hats and laden down with crackers. Each goblin seemed to be singing a different carol, and every one of them was out of tune.

Cheryl waved her wand and a banqueting table appeared at the far end of the Throne Room. It was laden with platters of turkey and bowls of stuffing and bread sauce, as well as Christmas puddings and iced Christmas cakes.

"Party time!" the goblins squealed in delight.

They fell onto the food with

enthusiasm, pulling crackers, telling jokes and gobbling down the yummy treats. Meanwhile, Jack Frost had leaped into the sleigh.

"Santa's grotto, here I come!" he whooped.

The reindeer shook their antlers and the sleigh rose into the air, turning towards the window.

Then there was a bright flash, and in the blink of an eye, the reindeer and the sleigh were on the other side of the window, galloping away into the night. Cheryl fluttered down to the girls. "You did it!" cried Kirsty happily. "*We* did it," Cheryl corrected her. "Without your help, I could never have got all the magical objects back in time."

"The goblins are warm and happy and Jack Frost is having his best Christmas ever," said Rachel. "It's perfect!"

"*Almost* perfect," Cheryl corrected her. "I still have to get you both home before midnight strikes!"

She threw her arms around them and hugged them tightly.

"You've saved Christmas," she said. "I can never thank you enough. But I can make sure that you have a wonderful, merry Christmas!"

"Happy Christmas!" said Kirsty and Rachel, hugging her back.

A fountain of golden fairy dust erupted from Cheryl's wand and showered down on the girls. They were dazzled by the sparkles, and when their vision cleared, they were back in their cosy room in Christmas Cabin.

The presents Rachel hadn't finished wrapping earlier were now beautifully wrapped and labelled.

"Cheryl must have done that," said
Kirsty as they changed into their pyjamas.
"How kind of her."

"Hasn't it been a wonderful Christmas
adventure?" said Rachel, leaning over to
draw the curtains. "And I'm so excited
about Christmas Day— Oh! Kirsty,
look!"

Kirsty dashed over to the window
as Rachel flung it open. Silhouetted
against the full moon was Santa's sleigh!

The girls breathed in the crisp night air as they gazed upwards, their heads pressed close together. They could see the outline of a huge pile of presents in the back of the sleigh. A big man with a bushy beard and a red-and-white hat held the reins, and beside him they could see a thin, spiky-looking figure.

As the sleigh disappeared into the distance, a voice carried to them on the night air.

"Ho ho ho!"

"That's Jack Frost!" said Rachel in delight.

The best friends looked at each other and smiled.

"Come on, let's go to bed and wait for Santa to visit *us*," said Kirsty. "Everyone will have a happy Christmas after all!"

The Showtime Fairies

Now the girls have helped Cheryl the
Christmas Tree Fairy, it's time for them
to help out the Showtime Fairies!
The first fairy they meet is

Madison the Magic
Show Fairy

Read on for an exclusive extract...

All the Fun of the Fair!

Rachel Walker gazed excitedly out of the car window, as her mum parked. A short distance away she could see a helter-skelter, a spinning tea-cups ride, the dodgems, and all sorts of sideshows and stalls. "This is going to be fun!" she said to her best friend, Kirsty Tate, who was sitting next to her in the back seat.

Kirsty grinned. "It looks great," she said, her eyes shining. Kirsty had come to stay at Rachel's house for a whole week during the October half-term, and it was lovely to be with Rachel again. The girls always had the best time when they were together…and the most exciting fairy adventures, too! They had helped the fairies in many different ways before, although their parents and other friends had no idea about their amazing secret.

"There," Mrs Walker said, switching off the engine. She turned to smile at the girls. "Do you want me to come in with you?"

Rachel shook her head. "We'll be fine, Mum," she said. "We're meeting Holly near the helter-skelter in ten minutes, so we'll go straight there."

"OK," said Mrs Walker. "I'll be back here at three o'clock to pick you up. Have a good time."

"We will," Kirsty said politely. "Thanks, Mrs Walker. See you later."

The girls went through the park gates. There was a sign advertising the 'Tippington Variety Show', which was to be held at the end of the week, and Rachel pointed at it. "Mum's got us tickets for that as a treat," she said.

"A variety show... That's one with lots of different kinds of acts on, isn't it?" Kirsty asked.

Rachel nodded. "Yes," she said. "And they're holding auditions for the acts all this week. Today they're auditioning for magicians. Lots of the schools around here have put forward performers, and the best one will get to appear in the Variety Show next Saturday. My friend Holly's been picked from our school to audition, so I said we'd cheer her on."

The girls walked through the park

together. It was a breezy autumn day, and lots of people were enjoying the rides, or trying their luck on the stalls. They passed a hook-a-duck stall, a big rollercoaster and dodgems, and could smell sweet candy floss, salty chips and frying onions.

The auditions were taking place in a tent next to the helter-skelter. "There's Holly," Rachel said waving at her. "Wait till you see her magic tricks, Kirsty, she's really good. She's been practising non-stop lately."

Kirsty grinned. "And magic is something we know all about," she said. "I wonder if we'll meet any more fairies this holiday?"

"I hope so," Rachel said, lowering her voice as they approached Holly. "Oh, Kirsty, I really hope so!"

Win Rainbow Magic goodies!

There are eight baubles in
Cheryl the Christmas Tree Fairy and every one has
a secret letter in it. Find all eight letters and rearrange
them to make a special Christmas word, then send it
to us. Each month we will put the entries into a draw
and select one winner to receive a special Christmas
gift from the fairies!

Send your entry on a postcard to Rainbow Magic
Cheryl Competition, Orchard Books, 338 Euston Road,
London NW1 3BH. Australian readers should write to
Hachette Children's Books, Level 17/207 Kent Street,
Sydney, NSW 2000.

New Zealand readers should write to Rainbow
Magic Competition, 4 Whetu Place, Mairangi Bay,
Auckland, NZ. Don't forget to include your name
and address. Only one entry per child.
Final draw: 31st October 2011

Good luck!

If you liked this story
you'll love these other fantastic
Rainbow Magic books!

Out now!

**The Rainbow Magic
Party Fairies Treasury**
978-1-408-30914-8